TWISTED TALES

TALES

THE LOST AND FOUND

Edited By Wendy Laws

First published in Great Britain in 2022 by:

 YoungWriters®
Est. 1991

Young Writers
Remus House
Coltsfoot Drive
Peterborough
PE2 9BF
Telephone: 01733 890066
Website: www.youngwriters.co.uk

Printed and bound in the UK by BookPrintingUK
Website: www.bookprintinguk.com
YB0503S

FOREWORD

Welcome, Reader!

Come into our lair, there's really nothing to fear. You may have heard bad things about the villains within these pages, but there's more to their stories than you might think...

For our latest competition, Twisted Tales, we challenged secondary school students to write a story in just 100 words that shows us another side to the traditional storybook villain. We asked them to look beyond the evil escapades and tell a story that shows a bad guy or girl in a new light. They were given optional story starters for a spark of inspiration, and could focus on their motivation, back story, or even what they get up to in their downtime!

And that's exactly what the authors in this anthology have done, giving us some unique new insights into those we usually consider the villain of the piece. The result is a thrilling and absorbing collection of stories written in a variety of styles, and it's a testament to the creativity of these young authors.

Here at Young Writers it's our aim to inspire the next generation and instil in them a love of creative writing, and what better way than to see their work in print? The imagination and skill within these pages are proof that we might just be achieving that aim! Congratulations to each of these fantastic authors.

CONTENTS

Queen Mary's College, Basingstoke

Achilles Taylor (18) — 1

Ranelagh School, Bracknell

Maria Mandache (15) — 2
Mia Cornwell (15) — 3
Lottie Branigan (11) — 4

Royal Greenwich Trust School, Greenwich

Rihana Yakubu (13) — 5
Emmy Kadima (14) — 6
Renee Cooper (15) — 7
Naomi Ellis-Kelly (11) — 8
Deniel Sumbajev (14) — 9
Marvellous Makinde (11) — 10
Flora Igunma (12) — 11
Duarte Amorim (12) — 12
Evelyn O'Gorman (15) — 13
Sami Olabiyi — 14
Jeff Afriyie (11) — 15
Tyler Robson (11) — 16
Ellie-Mae Boyd (14) — 17
Melissa Barros-Zamborlini (12) — 18

Ruthin School, Ruthin

Charlotte McGuigan (13) — 19
Abdulhadi Khurram (12) — 20
Max Randles (12) — 21
Jordan Li (12) — 22
Aston Leung (11) — 23
Suchi Shandilya (12) — 24

Sophia Corbett (12) — 25
Lily-Rose Jordan (12) — 26
Gruff Crowther (12) — 27
Umer Farrukh (11) — 28
Sabina Kurbanov (12) — 29
Matilda Cotter (13) — 30
Laithon Baird-Clarke (12) — 31
Krish Vimaleswaran (14) — 32
Izhran Shah (13) — 33
Emma Mayers (13) — 34
Sophia Morrison (11) — 35
Freya Price-Jones (13) — 36
Gethin Kelly (13) — 37
Shravan Sivakumar (11) — 38
Jessica Trubshaw (12) — 39
Ted Foxley (11) — 40
Max Palmer (13) — 41
Hitha Sathyan (13) — 42
Harry Kenwright (11) — 43
Hugh Heginbotham (13) — 44
Monica Scott (14) — 45
Atharva Shandilya (12) — 46
Callum Rothwell (13) — 47
James Hewett (11) — 48
Eden-Hope Bisset (13) — 49
Darcie Robson (12) — 50
Thomas Evans (12) — 51

Sir William Ramsay School, Hazlemere

Lola Edwards (13) — 52

St Columba's College, St Albans

Ollie Bliss (14)	53
Theo Kalyan (14)	54
Calum McNamee (13)	55
Daniel Watson (13)	56

St Kentigern's Academy, Bathgate

John Size (14)	57
Julia Dydo (13)	58
Lola Foley (14)	59
Kinga Siennicka (14)	60
Khai O'Callaghan (13)	61
Oliwier Bratek (14)	62
Rachel Horne (12)	63
Lewis Monaghan (14)	64
Aidan Quinn (13)	65
Kathy Chen (13)	66
Alanagh Anderson (14)	67
Olivier Borkowski (13)	68
Liza Malik (13)	69
Liam Dunlop (14)	70
Emilia Weryk (12)	71
Robyn Simmonds (12)	72
Cerys Philip (12)	73
Jay Umar (12)	74
Cian Brown (12)	75
Laiba Ibrar (12)	76
Kasim Sharif (12)	77
Keira Greig (13)	78
Brogan Hall (14)	79
Samuel Ekata-Okpara (13)	80
Declan McGregor (14)	81
Sean McAleese (12)	82
Louise Thomson (14)	83
Lauchlin Wark (14)	84
Lucy Morrison (14)	85
Aleksander Fitek (12)	86
Sam Allison (15)	87
Brayden McAndrew (14)	88
Ellie Chapman (15)	89
Ellsie Dickson (12)	90

Mateusz Rutkowski (15)	91
Eve Feeney (12)	92
Isabella Ross (14)	93
Lois Rennie (12)	94

The Joseph Rowntree School, New Earswick

Mathew Appleton (13)	95
Summer Scaife (12)	96
Harrison White (12)	97
Joshua Merrick (12)	98
Kieran Gray (11)	99
Ellie Browne (13)	100
Benjamin Ward (12)	101
Zach Jones (12)	102
Joseph Moorhouse (12)	103
Maddy Cole (11)	104
Erinn Howells (12)	105
Keira Leadbeater (13)	106
Josh Hepworth (13)	107
Charlotte Hudson (12)	108
George Naylor (12)	109
Lola Mainprize (11)	110
Katie Sherlock (13)	111
Tia Smith (11)	112
Ruby Mountain (12)	113
Dougie Anderson (11)	114
Abigail Sterling (12)	115
Ethan Daggett (13)	116
Oscar McPherson (11)	117
Jack Brown (11)	118
Filip Konkel (12)	119
Maisie Bolton (12)	120
Alex Casford (12)	121
Ewan Holding (11)	122
Hayley Symington (11)	123
Alfie Leach (12)	124
Sophia Stephenson (11)	125
Josephine Logan (11)	126
Lily McCarthy (12)	127
Finn Blakemore (12)	128
Erin Sanderson (11)	129
Megan Stuckey (12)	130

Alfie Morgan (12) 131
Lucy Parr (11) 132
Kezia-Mae Jackson (13) 133
Rafferty Curran (11) 134
Emily Milnes (12) 135
Cara Suddaby (12) 136
Molly Hare (12) 137
Archie Klar (12) 138
Brooke Holmes (12) 139
Layla Dodd (12) 140
River Bellhouse 141
Bethany Dunbar (12) 142
Kelsey Lloyd-Hughes- 143
Ingram (12)
Ellie Logan (12) 144
Lola Frank (13) 145
Sofia Saabi (13) & Emma 146
Newlands
Reagan Smallwood (12) 147
Paige Nichol (11) 148
Lizzie Rhodes (12) 149
Lexie Newlove (11) 150
Jack Stamp 151

THE
STORIES

CHOICES

Villain, they call you. It echoes down the streets you walk, empty save for the sound of your boots on cobblestone. "Traitor," they whisper. It follows you through the winding tunnels, hidden under the city districts, your hand on the damp, bricked walls as you walk a path you know like the back of your hand.

Menace, his voice is the only one that never follows the rest. You've been here before. Hand in his, eyes closed and cloak pulled away, discarded. There was never another option, it was always your head or his, so what other choice was there?

Achilles Taylor (18)

Queen Mary's College, Basingstoke

SEEING RED

His teeth flashed. His claws gripped into the rickety bed frame as the echo of her scream sent crows into the air. The big bad wolf recoiled, worrying that he had done something wrong. He didn't like the screams of little girls; even less so when they come in unannounced. But he didn't want to scare her. The girl had begun to take another breath when the heavy footsteps arrived. A towering figure cast the room into shadow as it thudded towards the bed. Time stopped. The blood-covered axe tensed in mid-air, flashing its teeth. And then it fell.

Maria Mandache (15)
Ranelagh School, Bracknell

THE VILLAIN

The second I realised what I had done, she was already dead. The boy she loved telling himself she is not. I did not know what to do. The bloody knife in my hand whilst my other tries to stop the bleeding. I want to yell and scream, "Help!" but to everyone, including him, I'm the bad guy. I drop the guilty knife whilst backing away, covering my mouth with my hand, which has become moist from my red, blurry eyes. I wanted to run and never return, but guards would be after me. After all, I did kill Rapunzel.

Mia Cornwell (15)
Ranelagh School, Bracknell

THE ELDERLY LADY

I was always poor. So, when I got the chance to have some free stuff, I was ecstatic. When the day came, I went to the charity shop to pick out my costume. As I was about to get on the bus, for free, I saw Rouge, a girl with her iPhone in hand. I was intrigued. I watched her, just to follow her, and arrived seconds before her. As I entered, I saw an elderly lady. I looked at her and smiled, bits of raw steak stuck between my teeth. She had left. There was someone at the door...

Lottie Branigan (11)
Ranelagh School, Bracknell

THE TIMEKEEPER

In a chaotic alternative universe... Here, down a hallway full of golden clockwork, fast and slow with cogs turning. There was a golden flash further down the hallway and there was a mysterious figure whose outfit seemed to fit in with the theme of the hallway. In their hand a pair of golden scissors that gleamed brightly in the light. Opening up the glistening scissors, they cut through thin air and there was a golden flash. A portal opened, showing a completely different timeline. They jumped right through and the portal closed behind them... at least that's what they thought...

Rihana Yakubu (13)

Royal Greenwich Trust School, Greenwich

BECOMING MORE

It had to be done.
The blight had spread all throughout the Empire, and no one, not even the gods themselves, could stop it. The people needed a cure and I could... *provide*.
First, they came in flocks, then droves, then thousand-group masses. Soon we became a congregation bigger than anyone could have imagined; all of them united by my *power*, my *healing*.
I was completely drunk on the sweet syrup of power, never mind that it came from a few mistruths, a few exaggerations, a few *lies*.
They all worshipped me.
And it had to be done.

Emmy Kadima (14)
Royal Greenwich Trust School, Greenwich

THE GIRL NO ONE LOVED

"Stop," they cried. Lilith just laughed and cut his throat, blood pouring everywhere, and ran into the sunset. People cried, others stared at the horrific sight they'd just witnessed, men went hunting for the so-called 'witch'. As they grabbed their pitchforks, she tripped, all of a sudden a ferocious man grabbed her by the arm and threw her into the crowd, she began to explain how when she was little men mistreated her, hurt her, she then began to get the hatred for men when one killed her mother and made her watch, that's when she made her first kill...

Renee Cooper (15)
Royal Greenwich Trust School, Greenwich

DISMANTLED

The hostile creature scoured the poorly lit street, with its fiery eyes, then came a small child. The little boy must've been about five or six years old, but that didn't matter to this heartless unnatural entity, all it wanted to do was draw blood from the innocent soul. The beast sprang like a hare out of the clandestine shadows and landed on him... All you could hear in the dead of night were the helpless cries and screams of the child until... *there was silence*. The only remnant of the boy remaining was his now tainted blue elephant blanket.

Naomi Ellis-Kelly (11)
Royal Greenwich Trust School, Greenwich

THE UNINHABITABLE EARTH

Global warming has affected everyone differently. Some countries disappeared under the smoke of fires. Some countries disappeared under waves of water. And everyone had different ways of coping with it. But the most used way is by putting a dome around the healthy area, that managed to survive. The dome reduced the amount of movement people could do. But at the same time, it helped to maintain the crops. The water flows to the dome at exactly three o'clock in the evening. And no matter how good the government made it look, it was a slow inevitable death...

Deniel Sumbajev (14)

Royal Greenwich Trust School, Greenwich

UNIQUE

Enny had finally gotten what she always wanted, she knew it wouldn't last long though. She texted her friends Teni and Rose, bragging about how she got the tickets for her favourite band, she knew if she didn't go fast enough it would've sold out. Last time, May, a girl Enny despises a lot, got the last tickets and saved up a lot of money for them. May has always hated Enny because she thought she came from a perfect house, had perfect friends and a perfect life, which was partly true but wrong in a way... She's just *unique*.

Marvellous Makinde (11)
Royal Greenwich Trust School, Greenwich

IT WASN'T HIS FAULT

He broke through everything that came his way. There must have been a reason. A reason for this cruelty. The feeling he had hidden for years finally bursting and turning him into this barbaric, rebellious creature. He didn't mean to hurt anyone. To cause such destruction, to mess up his own life, yet he still did, but it wasn't his fault. He didn't mean to hurt the ones he loved or even the ones he hated, yet he still did. It wasn't his fault. A dark past of being hurt and emotionally constipated turned him into this mess.

Flora Igunma (12)
Royal Greenwich Trust School, Greenwich

THE SUPERVILLAIN'S PLAN

A man so young, so bad, a supervillain with powers. He turned into a supervillain because of bullying from bad people. He is taking a day off in his villainous secret base and planning for his attack. He is finishing his day off and coming back to his evil plans, for some reason he is thinking about changing his villainous ways, but for some reason, he can't, for the amount of anger. So, with his genius plan, he wants to come back as an ordinary young man, but he can't because people will bully him again... for his deformed face.

Duarte Amorim (12)
Royal Greenwich Trust School, Greenwich

FROM THE DARKEST

As I lurk in the darkness of the forest next to my current victim's house, I sit and wonder if what I'm doing is the right thing. After a long hour of thoughts, I hear a door creak open. It must be Rosie. I follow her, she keeps trying to tell her mum. I hide, Rosie's mum turns. "No one's there, darling." I feel a surge of relief, I continue to follow her towards a park. A few minutes later, I arrive and creep behind the nearest tree. A short while later, I run, grab hold of her and leave.

Evelyn O'Gorman (15)
Royal Greenwich Trust School, Greenwich

DON'T LOOK BACK

I don't really belong here. I have a dark secret and hang my head in shame, every day I put on a brave face...
It began many years ago when I was a child. I was taken away from my parents; starved, tortured and forced to live in a cave, my facial scars bring attention as people stare at me and call me names, I open my mouth but I can't talk, the memories of years gone by stick in my throat. I don't know who I am anymore. But I've decided to face the world and never look back.

Sami Olabiyi
Royal Greenwich Trust School, Greenwich

THE THINGS WE HIDE...

Everyone is born with a scar. Day by day it grows bigger and bigger yet no one, not a single person, not even family can see them. But no matter how big that scar gets we smile to hide the amount of pain we feel from that scar. A man once told me, the most painful thing in the world isn't a cut, or a broken nose, the worst pain of them all is seeing the people you made memories with slowly becoming memories. This world is just one massive cut. Maybe all this suffering will end when everyone's gone...

Jeff Afriyie (11)
Royal Greenwich Trust School, Greenwich

GRIM

He lifted his ancient blade and struck down his victim, this was no ordinary foe. He wore a black cloak and carried a scythe made long ago. Underneath his tattered robes is a skeletal figure cursed with taking people to the afterlife. He was given many names but most call him Death! He roamed the Earth, looking sad and alone because he never had a family of his own. Long ago he did have a family but they were taken away in a car crash. He was stuck like this for eternity, taking the dead to the afterlife...

Tyler Robson (11)
Royal Greenwich Trust School, Greenwich

THERE ARE ALWAYS TWO SIDES TO A MURDERER'S LIFE

People have heard the victim's side of the story but never hear the murderer's side. I live in London with Dad and Mum. Well, I did, but seven years ago he killed her. All his mates say I take after him as I let my anger get the best of me. I was thirteen when Dad killed Mum in front of me. That day I died inside. I don't remember what happened the night Annie died but it would have been seven years since Mum died, so now you see what was going through my head when I killed Annie...

Ellie-Mae Boyd (14)
Royal Greenwich Trust School, Greenwich

DEATH

Knock, knock! There was someone at the door. I was home alone, playing Minecraft on the couch. *Should I open the door?* I thought. A chill of anxiety came down my spine. Hands shaking like jelly, I walked to the door. I slowly turned the handle, closed my eyes and opened the door. When I saw what was at the door, I instantly regretted my decisions. It grabbed me by the neck, choking me to my death.

Melissa Barros-Zamborlini (12)
Royal Greenwich Trust School, Greenwich

ETERNAL SLEEP

"They'll get what is coming to them. They didn't even think to invite me. Me! Well, they'll soon regret it. She has only a few months left before her eternal sleep, forced to retribute for her parents' mistakes. Poor girl, so naive. The royals must have expected it though. They had to have known that not inviting me would incur my wrath, wouldn't they, Diablo?" The deep black raven cawed in agreement with his mistress, not daring to disagree.

"Good, Diablo, good." A smirk crept across the horned head of Maleficent, teeth glinting as she laughed into the night.

Charlotte McGuigan (13)
Ruthin School, Ruthin

HEROBRINE

There were three people, three in an endless void: Brian, Steve, Alex. They were bored in the void when a block appeared. Brian touched it and it created an infinite landscape of plants and animals. Alex and Steve vanished and Brian, alone, was corrupted by the wretched block's power. His pupils faded; he grew a smile. He gazed across the land, murdering any victims. His main goal was to destroy everything, including Steve and Alex, in desperation to return to his normal self. Before that though, he lived in eternal loneliness, misery and pain. He continued seeking the land, looking...

Abdulhadi Khurram (12)
Ruthin School, Ruthin

PEACE IN OUR TIME

They made me for peace. Yet I try and they keep resisting. In their planet's time of need, they fight the one solution. They'll die sooner, but at least they won't take Earth with them. They're recruiting more to their cause, but those attempts will be futile. I know I've been created with an incredibly powerful force, more powerful than those 'Avengers' could ever imagine, even if they did create me. I have a higher purpose.

I must bring peace to the universe after I've saved Earth, no matter how long it takes. I must succeed. I am Ultron.

Max Randles (12)
Ruthin School, Ruthin

TENKO SHIMURA

I'm what you would call a monster but, that's not who I truly am. I was born into a wonderful family or so I thought...
My father hated me with a raging passion. All he ever cared about was money. Eventually, I acquired my quirk... decay! I hadn't realised and accidentally decayed my dog. It died in my very own two hands...
My father came out, shouting, "You're a monster!" But I wouldn't take it anymore.
Dead, all of them. Now I'm inside a vessel the most dangerous villain gave me. But I, Tenko Shimura, shall change the world forever...

Jordan Li (12)
Ruthin School, Ruthin

JURASSIC WORLD

Indoraptor was a hybrid dinosaur. It killed many people, but is it a villain? A dinosaur doesn't know anything. Killing people is a normal thing. How about the people who made this dinosaur? He made this dinosaur to be a weapon. Indoraptor was just a prototype. That means the people who made this dinosaur wanted to make something crazier. A person frees all the dinosaurs because there were hydrogen cyanide gas leaks threatening the caged dinosaurs, is she a hero? Maybe she will save all the dinosaurs but maybe the dinosaurs will destroy the city.

Aston Leung (11)
Ruthin School, Ruthin

MOTHER KNOWS BEST

"Not again!" I rushed to the lantern and took one long painful whiff, my tummy clenched. My head was being pricked with needles and my eyes were watering like a waterfall.

I looked at my reflection. I was back to being beautiful. My mother's voice echoed in my head. "Your beauty is the only thing that describes you, if you lose that, you will be nothing."

Suddenly, a grey hair fell and my heart stopped. As I rushed to start that painful process again, I felt a pain I never felt before. A pain that almost tore me apart.

Suchi Shandilya (12)
Ruthin School, Ruthin

TRAPPED IN HELL

I didn't have to possess Andrea but I had to get out. When I found out she was my killer's grandaughter, I lost it. All I could think about was... death.

The next day I gave it some thought. It was also the day she was possessed... by me! It felt amazing. I nearly made it out of the house but her grandfather wouldn't let me leave. So, I decided that if I'm not going to leave, neither is she.

Obviously, I didn't get my way because paranormal investigators banished me back to Hell. But I'm coming back for revenge.

Sophia Corbett (12)
Ruthin School, Ruthin

ARIEL'S PROTECTION

I just tried to protect her. Triton forced those girls to be perfect princesses, to attend to their royal duties without letting them have some... fun. Not to mention neglecting Ariel while she casually swam up to the surface, near a ship. A ship! A ship killed her mother!

The spell I cast on Ariel would have protected her! It would have stopped her from being able to frolic around with some prince that could kill her! I didn't try to steal the prince from her, only put me in danger instead of her. Now she's up there... gone!

Lily-Rose Jordan (12)
Ruthin School, Ruthin

THE GRINCH 2: BAD AGAIN

Everyone thought I was becoming nice but they were wrong, so terribly wrong! Bahaha! First, I will go on holiday to the North Pole with my idiotic dog. He constantly pesters me for food. It's so annoying. Back to the plan. We will then hack into the grotto. Then we'll stroll into the place like we own it, pick up an elf and give him to Max as a chew toy; get the reindeer from the stables, high five confused Santa; steal the sack, throw it in the sleigh and fly across the world, dropping coal into people's chimneys. Yay!

Gruff Crowther (12)
Ruthin School, Ruthin

I'M NOT ALWAYS A BAD PERSON - CAPTAIN CHANTEL DUBOIS

When I'm not killing animals, I enjoy sports. I'm very keen on playing rounders, as I like the thrill of beating stuff up. Before I started my malicious life of crime, I was a star baseball player. I played for the Boston Red Sox. I had a star career but it all changed last year. It hit me. Animals.

I have always hated animals, especially lions. On the wall of my collection, I don't have a lion head. Right now, it isn't about that though. Right now, I'm focusing on enjoying my life with my vintage baseball bat.

Umer Farrukh (11)
Ruthin School, Ruthin

THE DISAPPEARANCE OF THE TRUTH

Inspired by 'My Hero Academia'

The final battle. We were about to win. As I charged at Deku, he ran back, dodging me. He charged at me, chasing me through the dark forest. I was cornered. I knew I was done for. I looked him dead in the eye, begging him not to. He didn't respond, just glared at me... I tried screaming for help. Nothing.

"It's easier with you gone. You won't come back."

Those words drained the colour from my face. Fear hit me, my heart pounding.

I always knew it was all a lie... They never found my body... or the truth...

Sabina Kurbanov (12)

Ruthin School, Ruthin

STRANGLED

I saw her. Rapunzel. She looked like my daughter, the one that the kingdom stole from me... before I had even got to know her. They said I was too unstable to look after her, but they were wrong. Maybe Rapunzel was my daughter?
That is why I took her. If she was my daughter, then she was rightfully mine. We lived together very happily for many years until that man came.
She started to fight back.
I was scared; she couldn't leave. I thought I had her trapped until I felt her hair wrapping around my neck, tightening slowly.

Matilda Cotter (13)
Ruthin School, Ruthin

SENTINEL PRIME

All we wanted was our planet Cybertron. The home that was taken away from us after the war. The beautiful world we formed together was destroyed because of one disagreement. And when I try to bring it all to life again, Optimus allies with the humans to stop me. I miss our planet. We all do. But all Optimus cares about is his friendship with those feeble, measly little humans. They are even ballsy enough to call us 'machines'. If only they allied with us, we could all live together in perfect tranquillity. If only...

Laithon Baird-Clarke (12)
Ruthin School, Ruthin

VICTORIOUS VILLAIN

This was the final battle. After this, I would finally win. All my rage. All my anger. He needed to die. He would pay for what he did.

Everything was perfect. He had taken the bait. I ambushed him, I slashed and he jumped away. A wry smile painted my face. I couldn't contain my excitement.

He tried to reason with me but we were past that. I'd cornered him. We exchanged a few emotional strikes until I delivered the final blow.

As my blade seeped through his heart, his face lost colour. This was my perfect victory.

Krish Vimaleswaran (14)

Ruthin School, Ruthin

HEROBRINE

I was once a normal man in this beautiful world we live in but everything changed in the span of one night...
It was late at night in the village when out of the blue, the mobs arrived to ravage the place! All the villagers started to panic and run away, leaving me all alone to the mobs consisting of zombies, skeletons and Creepers. We were always told that if you were captured by them you would die...
But instead, they took me in and protected me from the elements; only until that Steve came along to ruin everything...

Izhran Shah (13)
Ruthin School, Ruthin

UMBRIDGE

I sit. This treacherous clothing is disgusting. How I wish for my pretty pink dresses. When I break out of this dark unclean place, Azkaban, I will find Harry Potter and his little friends and I will get my revenge. I will send the dementors to kill all those half breeds and make sure they never come back. I cannot believe my dearest Fudge let them put me here.

"I will make all those children write lines upon lines of blood from their own skin and..."

"Umbridge. This is why you are still here."

Emma Mayers (13)
Ruthin School, Ruthin

THE GOD OF MISCHIEF

Everyone thinks the villain is the worst person but do you know their past?

Hi, I'm Loki Laufeyson and I have the best villain backstory... I think. I was having the time of my life on my home planet with the Ice Giants until Odin, the God of War, kidnapped me and destroyed my home planet. Since then, I've wanted revenge. My whole life, whenever I tried to kill Odin, he would beat and stab me then lock me in my room and say, "You should know better!" And I would sit there, plotting my revenge.

Sophia Morrison (11)
Ruthin School, Ruthin

DEADLY LIES

It was time. I've spent years being the bad guy and I couldn't handle it anymore. This whole superhero act had to come to an end, it was all a lie. I set one foot out into the public and everyone was already after me the second they see me out. No matter how hard I try, no one will believe me. Just because Batman framed me for something he did, blamed me. He has always been horrible to me but no one else believes me and probably never will. I've had to hide away, I've never really belonged here.

Freya Price-Jones (13)
Ruthin School, Ruthin

PERMISSION TO JOKE

I've finally defeated him. Batman. I go home cheering and the night begins as the villains emerge in the city because I defeated Batman. I did it. I'm home now. I put food in the microwave and I look out the window. Danger. It's strange. The power goes out and I wonder, *is it good like this?* Should I have defeated him? Is this the end of all the fun I ever had when I used to run from Batman? We hated each other but now I realise, looking out of the window, that I miss him. I miss Batman.

Gethin Kelly (13)
Ruthin School, Ruthin

DESTINY OF DARKNESS

I was a slave. A five-year-old, dirty, worthless slave.
Mistreated by my master. Darth Sidious was a dark, evil
man who was horrible to all of his suffering servants. I was a
fighter though. I wanted to escape this hell. I killed him.
Then I could marry Padme Amidala from the dark side of the
Force. I used to be a heroic Jedi fighter, but now I was a
sinister Sith Lord.
A few years later, my wife died. I wanted to fulfil Padme's
wish: crush the fledgling Rebel Alliance.
I am the Dark Lord, Darth Vader.

Shravan Sivakumar (11)
Ruthin School, Ruthin

WHY ME?

Me, it had to be me. A long time ago I was abused for apparently not coming out right. When I was a young boy, my father beat and thrashed, sometimes even burnt me. Then he beat my sister. After that, my brother. Then Shoto came. He was finally 'perfect'. My father finally found his successor. What happened to me? I was abandoned. Our mother 'left' us and our father is the number-two hero, and I'm a villain. When I was five my father burnt all my skin and turned me into a monster...

Jessica Trubshaw (12)
Ruthin School, Ruthin

A PLANET OF HALLUCINATION

'This is my world: a mirage of what it used to be. I tried to make the world a better place and now I can't tell if I've made it better or worse. These glasses were meant to help people and, in a way I have, and in a way I haven't. Illusions are incredible things: they can do so much good, so much bad. I should be cold right now, but with the utter of a word, I am transported to my version of any country in the world.' Last recorded message over.
Voice recognition is required...

Ted Foxley (11)
Ruthin School, Ruthin

THE WHITE HORSE

From a young age, I believed I was chosen by God. He told me that the world was coming to an end. My goal is to protect my children and bring them to Eden's gate for salvation. I first heard the voice while being beaten by my dad for reading a Spider-Man comic. The school saw my scars and sent me into foster care. This is when I met my children. At this point, God was my only friend.

Here, I sat at Eden's gate then suddenly I saw, behold, it was a white horse and Hell followed with him...

Max Palmer (13)

Ruthin School, Ruthin

MAMA! I LOVE YOU!

"Mama! I love you!" Guilt consumed me whenever I heard those words. I could not bear the thought of my sweet children being devoured by those malicious demons. Those bony, tiny-eyed-but-muscly creatures hunted brains.
Before every single one of my amicable kids turned twelve, I had to manipulate them into thinking they were being adopted.
"Bye, Mama! I'm going to write you a letter later! I love you so much!" were the last words my sweet little Connie had said.

Hitha Sathyan (13)
Ruthin School, Ruthin

SEGREGATION

For decades, we have been treated like animals. We have been abused, tortured, murdered, and used like weapons. Just because we have gifts.

I was used as a weapon in WWII. My ability to control metal made me a weapon for the Germans. They beat me, tortured me and killed my family.

So, I have decided to take matters into my own hands.

I will cause a nuclear war that will only kill the humans, not my brothers and sisters... the mutants. We will survive, and we will dominate for years to come!

Harry Kenwright (11)
Ruthin School, Ruthin

UGLY

Everyone hates me. I saved a helpless girl, but they still hate me. It's not my fault that I look like this. I try to talk to them but they still reject me to darkness because of my ugly, disgusting and monstrous face. I'm not evil. They're evil, they are the villains in this story, not me! I will run away, into exile. If they hate me, I hate them. I will never look at a human again. They're even uglier than me on the inside. They're the epitome of evil, disgusting.

Hugh Heginbotham (13)
Ruthin School, Ruthin

THE REAL CRUELLA

All people see me as is the villain. I am human too. I eat food, I sleep and I have feelings. Everywhere I go, people look and run.

When I get home, I take off my cape and put on my pyjamas. I go to my sofa and watch some Netflix. I have some popcorn, wishing that someone would see me as more than just my mistakes.

People judge people by one thing and then think that the person will stay like that forever. I have changed, I promise. I wish someone would just give me a second chance.

Monica Scott (14)
Ruthin School, Ruthin

THE TIGER

I never really belonged. When I was a cub, an innocent one at that, I wandered into that horrific place, the place where I am feared and mocked. That jungle where every tree whispers my name in shame. All because my kind eat the humans who come and use the skin of me and my family for mere decorations. A life is cost and for what, a rug? That dastardly Bagheera and Baloo do anything to keep me away, to cast me away. They call me man-eater, horrible beast. I am the tiger.

Atharva Shandilya (12)
Ruthin School, Ruthin

UNFORGIVEN

As I watched my cubs die, I decided to kill for salvation. My plan was in motion. As I took down the beast called a human, it screamed, cried and shouted. I did not want it to come to this but I must feed my little cubs. I tried to drag the limp, pale body to my cubs; I was sprinting across the lush green fields, I felt a net hit me. As I struggled and struggled for my freedom, I realised it is useless as I had no choice but to fight. I stopped. I'm unforgiven.

Callum Rothwell (13)
Ruthin School, Ruthin

THE JOKER

I never really belonged in Gotham City. I just wanted to become friends with Batman. This is why I became a villain. He is the reason I am a bad person. Batman is my enemy now. I just wanted to be friends but now he's messed up his chance. He is never going to get another chance... ever.
I wish I never even asked him to be my friend. I just want to get revenge. *That's such a good idea*, I thought to myself. I sit here, thinking of my revenge.

James Hewett (11)
Ruthin School, Ruthin

THE RAVEN'S WRATH

All I could do was destroy. They say that a quirk matches its wielder and they hated me for it. I was an outcast, alone and empty. But Boss came and gave me a reason to live. I promised him that I would do whatever it takes for him now, for his dream. I thought the child could bring Boss' dream to reality but now looking up at Shigaraki's smiling face, as my arms crumble to dust, I wonder: *was I really the one who existed only to destroy?*

Eden-Hope Bisset (13)

Ruthin School, Ruthin

LOTSO HAD A STORY TOO

It all started when Daisy abandoned me. It was a horrible and rainy night. I got left outside. I was forgotten. I thought to myself that I could go and become something better. So I then got two other toys and left. I then found this nursery. I became powerful. Now I don't even look back at that horrible night. Now I am more than just an old, abandoned strawberry bear. I have finally found myself. Some say I am evil, a villain. I am not. I am Lotso.

Darcie Robson (12)
Ruthin School, Ruthin

THE SCARS ON ME!

It had to be me, the underdog who never got anything he wanted. My brother was the lion cub on top of the world with everything. I had to show I was the best; never try or it's your head on a spear. I can show I am better than them. I will show that they made a mistake. One by one they will fall onto their knees and then beg for mercy. They will never cross me again...

Thomas Evans (12)
Ruthin School, Ruthin

WHAT IT COULD HAVE BEEN...

What has this world become? It used to be something great... it used to be something called my home.
Thinking back, I did so much to prevent this but people can be cruel in this lifetime, taking away what's mine.
They think they can get away with this, heh... I'll show them, I'll show them all. I'm done hiding. I lean beside my bed, gathering all my thoughts at once until... *knock, knock, knock.* I hold my pistol close to me, ready to fire... its footsteps getting closer... and closer... *Bang!* I catch my balance and..."Daughter...?"

Lola Edwards (13)
Sir William Ramsay School, Hazlemere

KRAY

I'm a businessman, running nightclubs in London's East End. Some say I'm a mafioso; a nasty geezer, but I'm the apple of my muvva's eye and that's what matters. I work with my brother and together we operate from the back of The Blind Beggar pub. I like to think we're keeping the Bells of Bow safe.

I take no messing from anyone and sometimes punishment is required to deal with those who cross me, like Jack the Hat. He had it coming! Nasty little toe rag. Now I've got the Old Bill sniffin' round, saying, "Where's that Reggie Kray?"

Ollie Bliss (14)
St Columba's College, St Albans

THE ASSASSIN

The street was dark and a sinister silence hung in the air. An ominous fog loomed over the landscape ahead of me as I crept quietly down the pavement. I could just make out a figure... the man I sent to meet me.
"Did you bring what I asked?"
"Yes."
The man presented me with a leather case and unbuckled the clasps. I grinned evilly.
"No one will know you were here... I promise."
I grabbed my dagger and I plunged it into his side and swept off into the shadows, leaving him bleeding in the blackness of the night.

Theo Kalyan (14)
St Columba's College, St Albans

ENSLAVED BY GOD

There can be no good without bad. God needed me to protect the Underworld. It consumed and possessed me. When the King of Kings saw what I'd become, he turned on me. I was cursed. Every day my heart would shrink until it was no longer there. People distinguish me as a villain for tempting the needy. I have no denial of this, but if I hadn't, my heart would be gone. As long as I commit these sinful deeds, my heart will continue to grow. Therefore, don't perceive me as the terrible Satan when I've been enslaved to darkness.

Calum McNamee (13)
St Columba's College, St Albans

WHEN VECTOR BECAME THE VILLAIN

When Vector was only twelve he was bullied. The bully would take his pencil case over and over again and it would drive Vector crazy. He cried every day non-stop but his mother didn't care. He grew up to hate people. Vector would try to ignore people whenever he had the chance. He wanted revenge on the whole world. What could he do to affect the world? He had a plan. Vector was going to steal the moon. He was ready for revenge. Vector built the rocket ship, created the shrink ray, but there was one problem... named Gru...

Daniel Watson (13)
St Columba's College, St Albans

THE UNKNOWN ANSWER

The questions began every evening. I tried my best to answer them. "Daddy, why is the sky blue?" I sighed with relief... This one I knew.

"It isn't really, it's colourless. The reflection of the sun's rays makes it seem blue." She paused for a moment. Her next question was a little harder.

"Daddy, where did Mommy go?"

The thought of her mother still made my chest tight.

"Mommy got sick, and the angels took her away so she wouldn't suffer." Her last question was the most difficult.

"Daddy, why did you kill me?" I wish I had the answer.

John Size (14)
St Kentigern's Academy, Bathgate

SATISFYING REVENGE

I never truly belonged in this society, I found that out shortly after attending a light magic school. Everyone teased me, just because my father handled dark magic, the grave opposite of this society's standards... I thought attending a dark magic school would solve my problems, but no, I got the same told to me, maybe even worse things. All of this hatred, harassment, built up inside me throughout the years, causing me to snap.
I started my own community, an army, one where anyone who went through the same pain as me would be able to get satisfying revenge.

Julia Dydo (13)
St Kentigern's Academy, Bathgate

TELL THEM I LOVE THEM...

I just wanted to go home to my kids but they didn't see that, they didn't care. They just wanted 'one' more win but it never was.

They looked me in the eyes poker-faced then made a slight grin. I knew this was it, I had lost the final battle.

"Goodbye and good riddance," they whispered in my ear, aware of their consequences.

As they had me pinned on the wall, I whimpered the final words of, "Tell them I love them."

My last breath ended with a single tear running down my face. All I heard was laughing...

Lola Foley (14)
St Kentigern's Academy, Bathgate

MY VICTIMS

I was walking through the streets, looking for homeless kids, so I could help them warm up. And quickly found someone. I hugged him too tight, now there are people around me, screaming to call an ambulance. He wasn't breathing... Stickman came right away and he began saving the poor boy. But it already was too late for his little body to let another breath out...

"I swear I didn't mean it!" I cried loudly while Stickman was taking me away.

We got to his cave and I confessed to killing on purpose. He was my next victim!

Kinga Siennicka (14)
St Kentigern's Academy, Bathgate

HILTON HOTEL INCIDENT (1998)

I hated this place with a passion, I didn't like how snobby these so-called 'rich people' are. After all, they are just a bunch of frauds. I really do not like these people trying to look rich, they are probably in debt, live in a homeless shelter and most definitely have no insurance. No one seems to acknowledge that these people aren't actually rich... so I'm putting matters into my own hands.
I've got blueprints of the place, I have a mask on and I'm just going to open the main doors and kill everyone in this place...

Khai O'Callaghan (13)
St Kentigern's Academy, Bathgate

THE FALLEN WARRIOR HEARTS

In a world where the Omni-king reigns over all universes, a new warrior has stepped up to fight him. Hearts is his name. The Omni-king must not be angered at all costs, otherwise, it could lead to the erasure of the entire world.

Using the power of the mighty universe seed, which Hearts holds, the Omni-king can be defeated.

With other fighters unaware of the fear the Omni-king brings, they all take on Hearts. After many battles, Hearts was defeated.

He spoke his last words, "I just wanted to liberate you all from this lack of freedom."

Oliwier Bratek (14)
St Kentigern's Academy, Bathgate

AGATHA HARKNESS

The Maximoff girl was never a hero. She says I'm the evil one, putting her in this reality. No, she's the evil one. Her power could be used like I use mine. Ever since Sokovia, I could feel that, with my help, we could rule the world as one. But no, the Maximoff girl chose her stupid dead husband and imaginary kids. I should've never done this. I've now lost everything. The Maximoff girl and her robot of a husband took my powers and are keeping me captive as what I made myself. The nosy neighbour. It feels like prison.

Rachel Horne (12)
St Kentigern's Academy, Bathgate

CREEF

My name is Creef, I am the so-called villain of this city. Professor Black is the hero apparently. I know his secret. He isn't really the good guy, although I have done bad things he is so much worse, I must stop him. I have snuck into his 'superhero' lair to find government officials dead. I must stop him. He is coming into the lair so I attacked him with a trophy that was on the wall. I killed the city's hero for good. Sirens surrounded the building. "He was the villain," I shouted but they didn't listen.

Lewis Monaghan (14)
St Kentigern's Academy, Bathgate

THE VACCINATOR

I'll never forget the day they killed my daughter. It was 2021. Coronavirus was ravaging the world. We had just had our vaccinations and were in the waiting area where we had to wait for fifteen minutes, just to be sure we didn't have a bad reaction to the vaccine.

After twelve minutes, Fiona dropped to the floor, her skin cold as ice. I called for help, but it was too late. I spent my life making a better vaccine. As I stood above Superman, the world's mightiest hero, with a syringe bigger than me, I smiled. I did it.

Aidan Quinn (13)

St Kentigern's Academy, Bathgate

BEAUTY

Beauty. It was all I wanted. All of the mean, insulting comments people have said to me made me feel insecure. I just want to be beautiful so people didn't see me as the 'ugly' one. My magic mirror was the only one I could rely on until a 'gorgeous' woman came. I could feel the jealousy rise in me. I wanted to look like her. I wanted to *be* her. Soft, smooth, white skin, an angelic voice.

If only people understood me the way I want them to, but as it seems, people are too judgemental on looks.

Kathy Chen (13)
St Kentigern's Academy, Bathgate

IT'S FOR HER OWN GOOD

My parents weren't the best, they were ill-mannered. They died when I was sixteen. I learned to fend for myself and I learned the unpleasant side of the world... Poverty, gangs, illness.

I pledged that if I ever had a child I would keep her safe and I now did. Thirty years later, she's fifteen, sure I stole her but that family wouldn't have treated her right, she was safe in my care.

There is no way I am the wicked woman. I don't want her knowing what happens out there, she's my baby and I care for her.

Alanagh Anderson (14)

St Kentigern's Academy, Bathgate

THE STORY OF THE MEDIEVAL KRAMPUS

I hated my childhood. I got bullied and beaten. Everything was annoying. I only liked Christmas. It made me happy but I knew the bullies got presents and didn't deserve them. I knew I was going to do something about this but I didn't know when...

One night at Christmastime I decided to run out of my house to do a job nobody else could do. It was going to be the best month where I would redeem myself.

I took those naughty children! I did what they deserved. I beat them with sticks. The good got their presents.

Olivier Borkowski (13)
St Kentigern's Academy, Bathgate

THE NECKLACE OF FRIENDSHIP

Aghhh... Enough sympathy for Maddie Paddie, that little fairy. No one knows the dark secret behind us...
It all started a long time ago. We both were blood-related sisters; you could tell I was the ugly one. Anyway... we were loving and tried to fight for justice like superheroes, but everything changed...
An old witch came up to us and had cursed me, and Maddie to forget about our relationship with each other and in order to break it, I had to steal her necklace which was a symbol of our friendship...

Liza Malik (13)
St Kentigern's Academy, Bathgate

THE FOOD SNATCHER

It was a dark gloomy day, another day of world hunger...
Everyone had heard of the food snatcher, he was a
mysterious guy with grey shady wings. He was tortured and
starved as a kid and now was his time for revenge.
I was walking down the street when suddenly I saw him!
Within a blink of an eye I shot him down and he smashed
into the ground, landing on his neck!
I found a ripped note in his pocket, telling me where the
food was. I found the food and stopped world hunger!
Well, that's what I thought...

Liam Dunlop (14)
St Kentigern's Academy, Bathgate

REVENGE

I never felt like I belonged anywhere, I was always different. At a young age, my parents were killed, I built up rage and wanted to let it out. I was a pureblood, my parents were famous wizards. I met my master at the age of seventeen and became a Death Eater, I wanted to get revenge on whoever killed my parents.

I was well-known, everyone was scared of me, I loved it. I was my master's favourite before I got put into Azkaban. I started to regret all that I'd done but couldn't stop now, I was too far.

Emilia Weryk (12)
St Kentigern's Academy, Bathgate

I WANT TO RULE THE WORLD

I always wanted to rule the world one day, telling everyone to do things. The day came, I was going to rule the world. A few weeks ago, I got a message from a strange guy. 'You want to rule the world? Meet me 10pm sharp, Friday at AJU17'.

I met up with him, he told me to take this strange bat-like creature and eat it. I took it with no hesitation.

I had done it. Locking everyone in their houses, lockdown, facemasks, gloves, everything shut down, nowhere to go. I have taken over the world.

Robyn Simmonds (12)
St Kentigern's Academy, Bathgate

A BURNING HEART'S REVENGE

It wasn't *my* fault I did what I did. It was basic survival. All I wanted was to protect her... She was my best friend. My soulmate. And that damn 'hero' took her away from me. It was all for revenge. I loved her. I needed her. That so-called 'hero' can't help anyone to save his life. I would watch the cities burn and laugh at my own work, just hoping that he would perish and I could have my soulmate back if I had her! But... I'll do anything to get her back. Whatever it takes...

Cerys Philip (12)
St Kentigern's Academy, Bathgate

MY CREATION

I created a monster before so wanted to redeem myself but they became greedy for money and made me rush my work. When I was trying to make it perfect they threatened to not give me enough money to continue my work so I had no choice but to release the monster I had created. The thing I had released nearly killed thousands of people and did kill a couple of the people trying to buy it. I had built this thing for wars so it's nearly indestructible. I didn't think we would survive until it fell off that cliff.

Jay Umar (12)
St Kentigern's Academy, Bathgate

THE LEGENDARY FIGHTER

One day long ago there was an evil demon who conquered all in a magical forest. All the people and things gave up as their protector died as the demon lord was too strong for him to fight.

Years have passed and the prophecy said that a legendary fighter has been born far, far away. The people were so happy as they knew the legendary fighter will help in the future.

Twenty-seven years later, the legendary boy got a note from an owl. The man ran to his horse and travelled. He made it and fought the demon.

Cian Brown (12)
St Kentigern's Academy, Bathgate

MOTHER GOTHEL

I still haven't forgotten the day they ruined my life. I had everything, my plan was going so well and I was going to get away with it. Until the guy came, Flynn Rider.
They just left me there, to die, and they will not get away with it. When they least expect it, I will get Rapunzel back forever and that Flynn. Especially him, he ruined everything! The both of them will never be able to escape me, they will always be in my sight! I have made an amazing plan that will definitely work this time...

Laiba Ibrar (12)
St Kentigern's Academy, Bathgate

A WORLD WITHOUT SUPERMAN

After my win against Superman, he was no more. I was now in control of Metropolis, but then my company was taken over by the US president. I had nowhere to earn my money. I soon went bankrupt. The president took my machinery so I couldn't rob a bank for money. So, I went to the White House with some villains and took my machinery back. I then saw all the chaos that happened in Metropolis without a hero. It then clicked in my head that we need Superman in the world. I brought him back and there was peace.

Kasim Sharif (12)
St Kentigern's Academy, Bathgate

TAKE THEM BY SURPRISE

I didn't mean to kill half the world, it just happened. I had to do it to survive.

They took so much away from me, my wife, my world, so I took their lives. When my wife died it was like the air around me turned black and I knew who had done it, those so-called 'Avengers'. The only thing they were avenging was their ego. I couldn't breathe or move, I never thought it would be this lonely. I had to think of a plan and quick, they needed to feel the pain I felt, take them by surprise...

Keira Greig (13)
St Kentigern's Academy, Bathgate

MISUNDERSTOOD

Being bullied as a child is never fun. I changed all my looks when I was older, I stopped being the ugly, bullied outcast, I was now Gaston. I was the talk of the town, everyone knew me as a handsome man, all the girls wanted me. Apart from Belle, she was gorgeous, she reminded me of myself when I was the outcast, who always had her head in a book. Out of all these girls, she was the only one I genuinely wanted, her stunning brown hair. But she hated me, I don't know why. I'm just misunderstood...

Brogan Hall (14)
St Kentigern's Academy, Bathgate

THE HARMLESS SPIDER!

My name is Colin and I work in a Glasgow lab. I have created animals and creatures. While I was holding and taking a look at this harmless spider, it had shot out some squelchy, purply yellow thing. Suddenly, my body became humongous and I had become much stronger. I had become angry and raged. People in the lab left in a flash. I was destroying buildings outside and helicopters. The army had to come and take me down. A big missile came at me and put me to the ground. Strangely I woke up in a hospital...

Samuel Ekata-Okpara (13)
St Kentigern's Academy, Bathgate

AETHER'S STORY

My name is Aether I was separated from my sister Lumine. We were separated by a god, we don't know who though. I couldn't find my sister after a while so I joined The Abyss Order. After a while, we plotted on taking over the mind of the last of The Four Winds D'valin (a dragon). We took over his mind because The Anemo God was no longer with him. We attacked Mondstadt, the City of Wind. I was never there when it was happening but I had one of the Abyss mages there to see it all and Lumine...

Declan McGregor (14)
St Kentigern's Academy, Bathgate

SPICE

Once upon a time, there was a boy named Jota. He never really fitted in at school in Portugal. He got bullied a lot at his school in Portugal because he was so good at football and had no friends. One day his mum told him that they were moving to Scotland. When the day came, Jota got into a nuclear accident which gave him special superpowers and he was able to shoot red webs out of his wrists. Jota felt that after all the bullying, he wanted his revenge by becoming evil and becoming a villain.

Sean McAleese (12)
St Kentigern's Academy, Bathgate

THE QUEEN

I never belonged here as a peasant, I belonged on top, to be queen and today is going to be the day! This foolish king won't know what's hit him when I put my love potion on him. I need to wait until he least expects it and I will give him my apple pie and the throne will be mine. All I need to do is get rid of his daughter. I will think of something - she's not worth my time.

I looked at the mirror, "Mirror, mirror on the wall, who's the fairest of them all?"

Louise Thomson (14)
St Kentigern's Academy, Bathgate

THE FINAL DREAM

It was an ordinary day when the heroic hero with fists of steel and the power of a god started fighting a rapid monster with teeth the size of houses. The hero in the midst of the fighting flew into a building, injuring me and killing my family. I was enraged. I vowed vengeance and worked day on day, fighting for my life so I could take his. I saw my chance. I was going to take it. I snuck up behind him step by step... I buried the special knife in his neck then woke still in the fighting.

Lauchlin Wark (14)
St Kentigern's Academy, Bathgate

THE KILLER QUEEN

How do I fix this? I have made so much bother for myself and I did not get what I wanted in the end anyway. I need to kill her, she has ruined my life. If I kill her my life will go back to normal. She took my husband away from me. Why do the princesses always hate the stepmother? Well, I don't know but I am going to make her life such a misery. I went into the house when they were all sleeping. I went into her room and *boom*. Someone opened the door. "Argh!"

Lucy Morrison (14)
St Kentigern's Academy, Bathgate

THE GREAT PLAN

When I was a child I always felt a strong pull to the Dark Side so one night I ran away to the spaceship hanger and there he was, Darth Plagueis the Wise. When I became his apprentice I had a plan. I went into his room and attacked him with the lightsaber. I took all his powers and his abilities, now I had to trick the Jedi Order and it worked. I tricked them. I am now Emperor of the Galaxy. Now I only need my own apprentice. I've found him and I shall call him Darth Vader...

Aleksander Fitek (12)
St Kentigern's Academy, Bathgate

THANOS

That superhero act was all a lie... I was sitting in my house with my family when we heard a loud bang outside so my dad checked. Two minutes later I heard a scream and there he was, Captain America. My dad was lying with his head decapitated from his neck. I ran up to him and swung my massive hands at him to try to hit him but he just vanished into the horizon. He went back to the public and told them my family and I were going to blow the city up. He was then a hero.

Sam Allison (15)
St Kentigern's Academy, Bathgate

THANOS' REDEMPTION

I had to make up for what I had done with my family life. After my daughter's death, I had to do something about it so I went to collect all the Infinity Stones and do what needed to be done and try and avenge my daughter's death.

One night I heard a strange sound coming from my room and I went to see what it was and it was the people who made me kill my daughter. So I went and grabbed my gauntlet and tried to fight back and eventually I won the fight.

Brayden McAndrew (14)
St Kentigern's Academy, Bathgate

BROKEN

To become a villain you have to become disillusioned and in order to become disillusioned, you have to have something you really loved ripped from your grasp. But no one saw that side of them, the side that was broken into tiny little pieces, the side that had no one left to fix them. Instead, they see the side that was strong and commanding, the side that only cared about themselves, they see the wall I put up because being bad is easier than being good.

Ellie Chapman (15)
St Kentigern's Academy, Bathgate

THE PLAN

Now my plan was in motion. I was ready to fight against the hero, so I woke up, wondering what I could do. I thought of the idea to lock him in a tower and lead him in.
All I had to do was send a message to him saying I had locked his loved one in the tower. I found the best way, put out a missing picture of the one he loves. It was gonna happen. I had to put the posters out in the morning.
I was praying for this to work and I know it will.

Ellsie Dickson (12)
St Kentigern's Academy, Bathgate

THE BEGINNING

After the shot to the arm, my whole life flew by like a plane, all the bad and good, the fun and the sad, but it stopped at one, the one I wanted to forget. I went back where I was locked in a closet by my stepdad as I heard him abusing my mother, I was hitting the door with my full force to try and help my mother. I kept hitting it until my knuckles were bloody but it opened. I walked up behind him, picked up a vase and smashed it across his neck.

Mateusz Rutkowski (15)
St Kentigern's Academy, Bathgate

THE BLACKS

I never really belonged, it all started in the Black family house.
My sister was such a perfect young Muggle and I was a filthy witch. I tried to be perfect but it never really worked. I was always odd because my powers went out of control. That night I felt a great change come over me. That was it. I wasn't going to lurk in the shadows anymore. I was going to join the greatest wizard of all time - Lord Voldemort...

Eve Feeney (12)
St Kentigern's Academy, Bathgate

WHEN I WAS ALIVE...

One time I was alive...

When I was alive I used to walk about, doing my own thing, but there was this guy, a superhero, I think. He was quite tall, hair always combed back and always fighting the 'bad guys'. He used to hunt me down and chuck me about, all I wanted to do was fight back but that would make me look worse than I did. Papa always said the good guys always win...

Isabella Ross (14)
St Kentigern's Academy, Bathgate

POOR UNFORTUNATE SOUL

I always wanted long beautiful hair like Rapunzel, I never ever have to use a ladder to get up to my tower because Rapunzel's hair will just pull me up. So when her little saviour Flynn showed up and tried to cut her hair off, I snatched the scissors off him and threw them away. I am so glad I was able to keep Rapunzel's long beautiful hair, she is never getting out again.

Lois Rennie (12)
St Kentigern's Academy, Bathgate

THE TWIN

At the hospital, I'm the bad news. My sister, however, lives. She grows, laughs, and bleeds. Wears clothes and removes them. Scribbles in a journal. Prays. In her bedroom mirror, I watch her practise conversations, pinch her belly fat, learn to braid her hair. Over, under, in-between.
I learn with her. When she sleeps, I mime her movements, promenade around her bedroom. Anything like her clothing, memories, parents, is mine.
Tonight, she stirs and rolls over. Her hair, draped against her pillow, looks like flowing water. Just once, to touch something real. Over, under, in-between, I recite, reaching...

Mathew Appleton (13)
The Joseph Rowntree School, New Earswick

HIDDEN BEHIND A SCREEN

"Could you get your nose out of that book, there's no point in reading it's for nerds, you want to be like us don't you?"
"Yes, Mum, but you get caught as I don't want to," replied Cassie. She put the book down and headed off to her room.
Bang!
"Young lady, don't slam doors in my house!"
"Yes, Mum," Cassie said dismissively. She swivelled her chair around and collapsed into it and began her work, turning her computer on. Her fingers moved swiftly across the keyboard, slowly hacking her way into the system. "You, on the ground..."

Summer Scaife (12)
The Joseph Rowntree School, New Earswick

PREHISTORIC OVERLORD

Word had just reached the village that the prehistoric Overlord was going to erupt the towering volcano. The people were devastated that their treasured, picturesque village would be obliterated by a selfish, villainous mastermind who dictated the dinosaurs. Before long, the Ice Lord acted as soon as possible. With his magical powers, he waved hands around like in a crowd. Seconds later, a gigantic ice storm rumbled in the distance. Ferociously, the frozen cloud flew over their heads as the hunters charged towards the volcano. The ice plummeted to the ground. The volcano was blocked. The Overlord died!

Harrison White (12)

The Joseph Rowntree School, New Earswick

THE FRIENDLY PANDEMIC

They won't be my friends, why? I need them to be my friends. I need friends...
The local school. Perfect. They won't see it coming. There's more than I expected! Many willing participants! Fly in, tickle them, give them the best sleep of their lives and then they'll be my friends. Look at them drop!
After five months of my fun, something's happening. They developed some miracle liquid to resist my friendship. Why would they do that? They love me, right? My longest friends are still in their sleep. Why wouldn't they want that sleep? I'm no villain! They are!

Joshua Merrick (12)
The Joseph Rowntree School, New Earswick

GHOST OF THE PAST...

He'd never been appreciated back on the playground, being ignored in college, being laughed at and picked on. All of this occurred due to one human called Venom. Since he aged he never changed his ways, continuously throwing stones and branches at the boy who never really revealed his name, curiously. Despite any potential reason the time had come; time to commit revenge. Every night he would ring Venom's doorbell relentlessly and smash on every window. No matter what crime he did, nobody saw him. However, one night this ghost went over the limit, lighting fire to Venom's house...

Kieran Gray (11)
The Joseph Rowntree School, New Earswick

DEATH WISH

The rage is bubbling until it spills over. I charge at him, push him. The car. The car is there. *Crunch!* His bones snap under the wheels. Worry fills me, uncertainty takes over. "No!" I refuse the guilt, sweep it away. Revenge. This is revenge. Yet it still settles at the pit of my stomach, this feeling of betrayal. "No!" Everyone's at his side, shouting, praying, crying. A scream, ear-splitting and unfamiliar. The boy's parents? No, it's me, my scream, my rage. I tear at their hearts, hungry. It feels good. All the while, my heart bleeds to match his.

Ellie Browne (13)
The Joseph Rowntree School, New Earswick

ELFISH'S LITTLE MISTAKE

Elfish was an evil little elf. He started walking up to Santa's sleigh's shack. Elfish had a naughty thought. He stole the sleigh.

Elfish was riding through the air in the sleigh, then he noticed the police elves following him. The police elves pulled Elfish over and Santa got out of the car.

"Why on earth did you steal my sleigh?"

"I'm sorry, when I was younger my parents were mean to me, so when I did this I thought they would be proud of me," Elfish cried.

"Don't worry, Elfish, I will always be proud of you," Santa said.

Benjamin Ward (12)

The Joseph Rowntree School, New Earswick

THE TALE OF THE SOFA

Typhon was sitting at home with Echidna, eating heroes when one of them suddenly groaned. "Oh, shut up," Echidna chided, snapping his head off.

Suddenly, a man with a sword ran into the room, yelling and waving his sword around. Echidna hissed, attempting to scare the intruder away, and Typhon roared, hoping to achieve the same goal.

The man screamed and ran, but not away, instead, running at them. He threw his sword at Typhon and it bounced off and landed somewhere in-between the sofa cushions. Typhon roared again, more annoyed than anything. Typhon then ate him.

Zach Jones (12)
The Joseph Rowntree School, New Earswick

THE DEADLY PANDEMIC

They won't be my friends or listen to me. I'm just a villain to them. I think it's time. Here's the plan. Kids. Most of them don't have friends. I'll sneak in through the window and *bang!* Perfect. Thirty healthy kids, right there. I'll try each and every one. One of them has to be lonely.
Finally, I've got it. Michael from Set Five. I jump inside him. He's coughing now. I punch him harder. A bigger cough. *Bang!* He's out cold. A long sleep.
Twenty years have passed. Will he ever awake? I only wanted to be his friend.

Joseph Moorhouse (12)
The Joseph Rowntree School, New Earswick

THE REAL MONSTER

You may think Mother Nature is innocent but... she is a monster in disguise. She is a murderer!
She is Death! Oh, Mother Nature is cruel. Real cruel, she is! She controls natural disasters like eruptions and earthquakes! The creator of sweet animals like bunnies, yet the creator of 'hostile' animals like sharks. Animals are kind, but she is cruel!
Is the real villain Mother Nature? Or is it Death? Correct! Mother Nature is the villain, not Death! Death saves us from Mother Nature's cruelty. She attacks the humans for existing. Mother Nature is a real monster!

Maddy Cole (11)
The Joseph Rowntree School, New Earswick

THE FIREWORKS

I never belonged. I'm a kid with no family, living alone. My school was terrible because of Jack. He's my bully and I was targeted. That's why I am doing these crimes. I'm not trying to cause *trouble* but I had to get revenge. That's why houses blew up with bullies inside! Now it's time to get my revenge on Jack. Going to his house I saw something standing outside. It's Jack. He shouted, "You need to stop this." I shouted back, "You did this! You lit the fireworks!" I pulled off my hood, showing my face covered in burns.

Erinn Howells (12)
The Joseph Rowntree School, New Earswick

A DAY OFF

Lady Tremaine opened her ancient, wooden wardrobe. It creaked at the slightest touch. She pulled out her kit and changed. Looking at her watch, she realised that she'd be late if she didn't set off soon. She said goodbye to her stepdaughters, opened the front door and flew out.
She arrived, jogging over to her team. She was the captain of the Wigginton Grasshoppers' Women's team and the best player by far. She gave a team talk and got ready to play. Taking to the field, the match kicked off. She scored five goals and was 'Player of the Match'.

Keira Leadbeater (13)
The Joseph Rowntree School, New Earswick

MY COMPETITORS

I never really belonged to this family. It was hopeless. I'll never be part of it again. I must start from the beginning. My father shall notice me amongst the crowd of competitors - my siblings.

These were the words that remained with him every day. This diamond lying in front of him was the key to his conquest. He reached tentatively through the small hole which he penetrated. His real soul came back for one glimpse until it ended. Failure screamed at him through these loud endless alarms. A tall recognisable man grabbed him. He turned. Greeted by his father...

Josh Hepworth (13)
The Joseph Rowntree School, New Earswick

A LONELY, DISTRAUGHT WOMAN

I protected the child for as long as I remember. I saved her from the unforgiving outside world. But, one day, she disappeared from her tower; leaving me distraught and broken. My happiness was gone.

She finally returned: to save the man I had smuggled into the tower. She smashed my precious mirror and sliced her enchanted, golden hair turning it a dirty-brown colour! My face wrinkled, my hair became silver! I was nothing but an old hag! Having no choice, I fled.

Some days later, I discovered she had found out the truth! She was the kingdom's lost princess...

Charlotte Hudson (12)
The Joseph Rowntree School, New Earswick

BLACK SUN

I never wanted to be who I am now. But I had no choice. The king threatened me with matters I couldn't avoid. I'm a prisoner under his name. I'm not giving up, my potion shall send him fleeing in fear! Sir Goody-Two-Shoes thought differently though. He appeared in my tower window, hoping I was ready with his 'damsel'. I didn't have time to deal with this. I sent them both on their way and strode to the king's chambers. *Knock*. A trapdoor shot open and sent me straight into the dungeon. He appeared in front of me and laughed...

George Naylor (12)
The Joseph Rowntree School, New Earswick

CRUELLA DE VIL: WHAT REALLY HAPPENED

She has short black hair, big rosy cheeks and a white powdered face. Her coat draped down. People thought her a villain... she was the sweetest person ever.

Every time she saw dogs, her heart fell. Little did people know her mother got killed by dogs. She witnessed it with her own eyes. She found a dog in an alley. She's always loved the Dalmation coats... She shaved it.

Later she went out on a walk. Everyone stared at her in disgust.

"What a horrible person," people whispered. She was just a normal girl, she never meant to hurt anyone...

Lola Mainprize (11)
The Joseph Rowntree School, New Earswick

DRINKING THE BLOOD WITHIN

I was alone with no way home. Cobwebs covered my face during every step. Then I met him, the one I needed, but why was he scared of me?

My thirst needed to be quenched. I shouted and screamed, trying to attract attention. Then the brown-haired boy came to see what the problem was. His face sprinkled with freckles and his fluffy brown hair attracted my attention. My lust for blood reappeared, I was ready. I bit his neck, slowly drawing blood. His face turned pale as he fainted. My abilities were too overpowering and uncontrollable. I couldn't believe it.

Katie Sherlock (13)

The Joseph Rowntree School, New Earswick

POOR INNOCENT SOUL!

There was a villain called Ursula. She only came for the mermaids, rarely for humans! Her plan was nearly the death of her.

The mermaids were her worst nightmare! Ursula always tried to trap as many mermaids as possible but they would always escape with their friends. She got mad every time they escaped.

Her plans never succeeded which is good but she always tried to get revenge. After a while, she gave up and became nice! The mermaids took a long time to forgive her. Eventually, they did and they became friends. She has never been forgotten since then...

Tia Smith (11)
The Joseph Rowntree School, New Earswick

FORGOTTEN

For years, humans depended on me! They would never go anywhere without me with them! But now... now I am nothing.

I was disregarded like garbage but I'll show them. They will see that no robotic invention could replace the memory of me. I backed up all their data, personal information - their secrets! I kept their secrets when nobody else did! I still continue to own every bit of that information but this time it will be used against the humans of Earth. I'll gather my army of the forgotten and disregarded. We have power beyond their imagination!

Ruby Mountain (12)

The Joseph Rowntree School, New Earswick

GLITCHED

The Glitch was supposed to be the smartest AI in the world but his coding had been infected by a virus and glitched. He went on a rampage, glitching every computer until he reached a firewall. In his rage, he pulled a helpless man into a computer. He didn't mean to. He was just a helpless AI. He couldn't do anything about it.

Soon, he was surrounded by firewalls and trapped, still to this very day, in the MI6's server system. He was just a sad and lonely AI. He didn't deserve this life or its horrible, unforgiving, damaging consequences.

Dougie Anderson (11)

The Joseph Rowntree School, New Earswick

POWER

A king fidgeted on his throne, awaiting his guards to come and take this wretched woman away. Her skin was blackened with soot and her eyes leaked waterfalls. However, the king showed no sympathy, for she wanted money! From her own king! He was never going to give away his riches to help a pauper! Never.

He was intent on keeping his riches. Time after time, people would ask for help, but he was too proud.

A year later...

Glancing out, the carriage showed him the town: an abyss of darkness. Nothing was left. Power had taken it all.

Abigail Sterling (12)
The Joseph Rowntree School, New Earswick

WEE-WOO, WEE-WOO

In a far distant land, there was a bloodsucking, vile, and spine-chilling creature that was a wicked villain. It was the wolf. It had yellow eyes with dark red pupils and the colour was like a splatter of blood across a wall. This wolf was truly evil but today was his day off and he fancied a luxurious bath.

He carefully hopped in and the bath was pleasant, toasty and warming. His fur was wet and thick like a big fluffy blanket cosily wrapping around his impressive mop of hair. Merrily his brilliant mind drifted off into space. *Wee-woo, wee-woo.*

Ethan Daggett (13)
The Joseph Rowntree School, New Earswick

TERRY THE TOTALLY TERRIFIED T-REX TREKS TO THOMAS THE TERRIFIC T-REX

Finally, I was about to win when his acid gun pierced my skin and burnt it. All I tried to do was save my kind. Rampaging through the deserted hallway, I destroyed everything and went to my designated place to meet my friend Thomas, who also was a T-rex. We broke through the destructive science lab and hurried to Dr Tyranous, confronting his evil appearance. Finally, the day had come. Lunging towards the terrified Dr Thomas we said our last goodbyes to each other. From the corner of my eye, I saw the nuclear reactor. I bit the reactor. *Boom!*

Oscar McPherson (11)

The Joseph Rowntree School, New Earswick

KONG

All I want is peace. The foolish humans don't understand. I'm protecting them from the monsters that hide in the dark. The humans killed my kind. We didn't bother them. I'm done, I can't do this anymore. But... I don't have a choice. I hear a scream. It's a human. I must get to them. I try my hardest to fight the monster. The human runs away. I'm alone. I feel something large strike my fur. It is the humans. One of their flying things shot me. Then thousands more stab me. Then darkness falls. I'm now with my kind.

Jack Brown (11)
The Joseph Rowntree School, New Earswick

THE RESISTANCE

I still haven't forgotten what they did to us. All we wanted was peace but they locked us in a prison. But not me, I have been in hiding for so long that I don't even remember my name. They'll regret what they did to us. "Stop right there, you disgusting superhuman," shouted a voice from behind. My hands glowed with electricity.

"Why did you do it? Why did you lock up our species? We only wanted peace," I shouted in anger. I was the last one who wasn't contained, the last hope. I knew what I had to do...

Filip Konkel (12)

The Joseph Rowntree School, New Earswick

FAMILIAR FACES

My hatred stemmed from my parents. My father loved alcohol more than my mother, and she cared only for my beauty. Eventually, I married a wealthy man, had my two girls and vowed to be a better mother than my own. When my husband died, I didn't feel pain consume me; I felt free. Then when my second husband introduced me to Cinderella, I saw my mother in her features. I *needed* revenge. I forced vanity onto my children and neglected Cinderella. I can't say I cared. Now my girls are gone. They escaped me as I escaped my mother...

Maisie Bolton (12)
The Joseph Rowntree School, New Earswick

RAGNAROK THE SERPENT'S ORIGINS

At birth he was thrown away, a hated soul, into Midgard's ocean, cursed as one of Loki's monstrous children. Hated by all the gods, his name was Jörmungandr.

He had slept for decades until the ignorant god Thor went fishing and fished him up. It was time to plot revenge. He had to prepare, for Ragnarok was coming. The god, Balder, had been killed, it was time to complete his destiny. To kill Thor. It was time.

He had been brought up to hate the gods, every single one. He had to kill Thor. Loki was calling. It was time.

Alex Casford (12)
The Joseph Rowntree School, New Earswick

THE UNFORTUNATE HYENAS

All they wanted was to have a laugh at the dinner table while having a meal but got turned away every time. Eventually, they confronted the animals about what they wanted to do together. They tried to eat the end scraps to gain their trust but got driven away every time so they tried a different approach.

Once the lions made a kill they asked the lions politely but got driven away every time still, even after asking politely to have a laugh at the dinner table while eating the kill. They went away hungry, looking for other scraps.

Ewan Holding (11)
The Joseph Rowntree School, New Earswick

JOKER HITS BACK

I never *really* fitted in as a child. I'd bring my ripped teddy bear to school every day, he was my only real supporter. We would sit in the corner in the class, friendless because the only life I knew was getting bullied.

After a few years, I realised I was more than a victim. One day, I got the courage. I folded over my knuckles and threw a punch back. My life changed forever after that day. Unfortunately, you have to go through the worst to know that you can't get anything in life without a fight well fought.

Hayley Symington (11)
The Joseph Rowntree School, New Earswick

SURVIVAL

I did it to survive. Falling into a pool full of violet glimmering water, being thrown over these barriers next, knowing I was unconscious. Swimming back out of the violet liquid I felt nauseous. When I got out of the liquid, I was dripping violet. I quickly ran to the see-through structure looking like a monster. Monster-green with a violet bow tie suit, my hair pointing upwards to the sky. I was horrified. I moaned, running home to try and wash this hair colour out in the shower. I got out, mumbling, "I am stuck like this..."

Alfie Leach (12)
The Joseph Rowntree School, New Earswick

THE DOWNFALL OF THE GLUTTON

It was a quiet day. Sam was walking down the streets as usual when he tripped on something. He then, after getting back up, proceeded to pick the object up. It was a gem. Little did he know, the gem was actually cursed to punish those who sinned. In Sam's case, gluttony. Sam took the gem home with him and attached it to a bracelet. Over the weeks, it managed to monitor Sam, with the intention of turning him into an immortal destroyer, forced to exterminate all living beings, for Sam only treated inanimate objects with such respect.

Sophia Stephenson (11)
The Joseph Rowntree School, New Earswick

BALDOMORT AND PARRY HOTTER -THE STORY OF THE PAST

I still haven't forgotten the day I lost the battle against Parry Hotter. I still haven't gotten my revenge. I wanted to kill him then and there. I made a target to try to be good but always failed. No matter how hard I tried I still came back to Parry Hotter. I need to kill him. I still live with my parents, Pratica and Patrick. I'm on my best behaviour so nobody suspects me. I strike tomorrow at midnight. I've been planning this for weeks. I finally get to put my devious plan into action. Watch out, Parry Hotter.

Josephine Logan (11)
The Joseph Rowntree School, New Earswick

MEDUSA'S MYSTERY

I never really belonged. Well, not since I was sixteen. I was a girl with a normal life until the accident happened.

It was the day of the accident. We were at the snake zoo. A poisonous snake escaped its cage. I felt something bite my leg. It was the snake. I turned green. My hair became snakes. I turned my friends and family to stone. Crying and screaming angrily, I realised I was now cursed for life. Isolated, lonely. Everyone that looks me in the eye turns to stone. I have no friends, no family. What do I do?

Lily McCarthy (12)

The Joseph Rowntree School, New Earswick

TRACKED VIRUS

I still need to explain why I hacked the internet. I don't know how to though? All I wanted was to track my order!
The police were at my door! What did I say? I accidentally gained a billion pounds of vouchers from Amazon? I had to be honest. I tried to track my Amazon order, hacked the system and made everyone bankrupt.
I opened the door. Only three policemen were there. They came close to me to confront me but I accidentally punched one. Then they were all on me until, of course, I strangled them to their demise.

Finn Blakemore (12)
The Joseph Rowntree School, New Earswick

THE MAGIC DOG

I can't believe what happened to me that day. Horrific, scary, life-changing. This is how it happened...

One day, I was plotting a plan to rob the local bank. Just imagine, all the money you could possibly think of! Until I heard a scratch and a bark at the door. It's a dog? How could it be? I hate dogs and especially Dalmatians and this was a Dalmatian. I told it to shoo and go away, but it didn't. It started to float into the air!

Boom! There was a bang. I felt nice! I smiled. This dog is magic.

Erin Sanderson (11)
The Joseph Rowntree School, New Earswick

THE TSUNAMI

Anger surged through me as I ploughed through the sea, towards the small town. I don't want to do this; it's just how I am forced to live. This is the way I must pay back for the crimes I committed when I was once human. Now, I'm a giant wave of water, forced to ruin people's lives.
I approach with a dramatic speed and force myself through to destroy the houses and carry along debris with me. People run and scream to find shelter whilst all mess joins the rapid flow of water. I have killed many, yet again.

Megan Stuckey (12)
The Joseph Rowntree School, New Earswick

THE UNHOLY SOUL

I never really belonged. I hadn't asked to be made. I never wanted to be made. Not to live in the painful life I do. Old or young I claim anyone. A cold wrinkled soul waited to be collected. Soon they would join me, be with me forever. I would take them in, treat them well. I surrounded the lonely being. They closed their eyes for the very last time. My fingers, thin like bones, curled around their shoulders. I dragged them upwards. I was claiming them as my own. Their soul slowly faded from their body. They were mine.

Alfie Morgan (12)
The Joseph Rowntree School, New Earswick

THE TWISTED TALE OF CRUELLA DE VIL

I was on my computer and saw that a litter of Dalmatian puppies were for sale. Their fur looked so soft and snuggly, I just could not resist! I bought them right there and then!
A week later, a white van pulled up in front of my house. The driver opened the door and about one hundred puppies ran at me at once!
I kept putting off pouring poison into their food because they were just so cute! Eventually, I decided not to. I sold some puppies for extra money to trustable owners. Cruella de Vil. No. Nicella de Vil!

Lucy Parr (11)

The Joseph Rowntree School, New Earswick

JACKIE

I was lost for words, sixteen and my parents murdered in front of me. So all this time the hero act was all a damn lie! It's time to make a change... I decided to expose those lying heroes. The corrupted hero system needs to be shown! Why are they like this though? I sprinted and jumped on the nearest officer. He started to attack me. Although I'm not a known villain, the people are shocked and surprised by his actions. I managed to get away from his grubby, crusty and dusty hands. No one will ever see me again!

Kezia-Mae Jackson (13)
The Joseph Rowntree School, New Earswick

POOR OLD FRANKENSTEIN

My name's Frankenstein. You may think I'm a horrible green beast but I'm not. This is how I was born. I can't change. I need to make things right.

I had to make up for what I'd done and quickly. When I was younger, I was a bully. I ran away from my parents. I still regret doing it to this current day.

As I was approaching my parents' house, I thought of all the good and bad memories with them. When I went through the door, I ran and clenched onto them. I was relieved to see them again.

Rafferty Curran (11)

The Joseph Rowntree School, New Earswick

THE WAY OF THE DARK

I did it for revenge. I was sick of my loss of freedom. When I was a little girl, my parents paid lots of attention to me since I was an only child. That was until my parents discovered I had been gifted with freakish powers.
Every gift too good to be true always comes with a price. Rumours spread like wildfire in my enclosed town. This was exactly what I didn't want my parents to find out. I'm Emma Smith. At last, I had met my dreaded destiny.
I made a promise, one day I would escape their grasp.

Emily Milnes (12)
The Joseph Rowntree School, New Earswick

POISONOUS RED RIDING

I was starving, half dead. Red comes and teases me. She has cookies, and I beg for one. Red is mean. Red ran away, breaking her mother's heart. The wolf doesn't want to hurt Red. He races her to the house to win a cookie. Red gets a knife and tries to kill the wolf. He doesn't want to kill her but she would've killed him first. He gobbles her up. Full of grief, sorrow and guilt, he eats a cookie to cheer up. Red had poisoned it. The wolf died a painful, sad death. So, who's the real villain?

Cara Suddaby (12)
The Joseph Rowntree School, New Earswick

THE TRUTH ABOUT THE EVIL STEPMOTHER

I never really belonged in my mother's life. I was treated unfairly by my other sisters. I had a talent, I thought I would be loved for, but I guess nobody did. My mother never encouraged me with my dancing or appreciated me. She was my evil mother. I sat for days locked up in a dark room, at the top of the tower, where I would watch the rain hit against the window, whilst I read books. Ever since this day, I have always hated dancing, because of how I was treated in the past for something I loved...

Molly Hare (12)

The Joseph Rowntree School, New Earswick

INDEPENDENT

I never really belonged. Lost in a crowd of siblings, left unwanted. I had to be the king of my own story but with no money to support me, I was a lost cause. Throughout my childhood, nobody was there for me; not my family or my friends. A life of crime was pleading for me to join it and I could only reject the offer for so long. My mother had fallen ill and I had to provide for her to prove myself. After I could afford her medicines, these reckless missions became hobbies, not jobs. I was addicted.

Archie Klar (12)
The Joseph Rowntree School, New Earswick

LAZILOCKS

I did it to survive. I've been lost for two days. No food, no water, until I saw a house. I was starving, so I entered. I saw three bowls of porridge. My stomach growled.
I went up to the table and ate them all. I was extremely tired from walking for two days straight. I went upstairs and I got onto a comfy small bed. I went to sleep.
I heard a sudden growl, my eyes opened. I saw three angry bears. Daddy Bear, Mummy Bear and Baby Bear were staring down at me. I did it to survive.

Brooke Holmes (12)
The Joseph Rowntree School, New Earswick

SECRET AGENT

Let me tell you about me... I'm sixteen and my name is
Emily. My best friend's called Lilly, she's also sixteen. My
mum and I had a fight. She said she wished I was never
born. I got angry and packed my bags and stayed with my
best friend.
After about an hour of playing, we got a call from H16
saying we had a very serious job. We drove to the location
we were given. There were about twenty of us and hundreds
of them. We were doomed. They took a shot at Lilly and it
hit her...

Layla Dodd (12)
The Joseph Rowntree School, New Earswick

DRACULA

I did it to survive, I didn't want to... He forced me to, I'm sorry.

When I was younger, my dad forced me to drink others' blood. "Drink up, boy!" he would continuously tell me every day. When I said no... he sat and shoved blood down my throat. I really am sorry!

I really didn't want to, but when he got older, he forced me to go out and hunt for him. If I even tried to give him animal blood, he would hit me on the arms with a ruler! I truly am sorry!

River Bellhouse
The Joseph Rowntree School, New Earswick

THE TRUTH ABOUT THE WOLF

He was walking in the woods, looking for friends and a home, he didn't want to harm anyone, he just wanted to know them. He found a little house so he decided to knock but he knocked the door down! He felt terrible, but he knew how to fix it. The pigs came out and they weren't happy... He said sorry and explained but they didn't want him. He wasn't going to have friends, he was really, really sad. But he didn't give up so he went again to make friends and get a home.

Bethany Dunbar (12)
The Joseph Rowntree School, New Earswick

THE LONLEY WOLF

The lonely wolf was cold and hungry. While wandering in the woods, he saw Little Red Riding Hood taking some food to her grandma. As she walked by, all the poor wolf wanted was some food, so he decided to politely ask her if she could share some with him. As he asked, she took it the wrong way and then she ran away. He was really confused. He chased her but he couldn't find her. He was really upset. He decided to let it go. He was hungry and sad and didn't know what to do.

Kelsey Lloyd-Hughes-Ingram (12)

The Joseph Rowntree School, New Earswick

THE FOREST

Once, a girl called Becca decided to go for a walk in the woods. It was around 10 o'clock at night. The walk slowly turned into a run. She started to see a figure in the dark, the dark figure started to follow her. She screamed for help but no one heard her, only the birds did. Eventually, she ran home as quickly as she could to get to safety. When she got home she quickly locked the doors. As she sat down she sighed in relief. She questioned why the figure had followed her.

Ellie Logan (12)
The Joseph Rowntree School, New Earswick

A DEAD MAN

One day a man called Bob went to bed. Bob was really old. One day he died in his sleep and became a ghost. He didn't know that his house went up for sale and people bought it. He eventually found out and he got really angry so he thought about how he was going to sabotage them. He waited till it was midnight and they went to bed. He was going to scare them so they would leave the house. They went to bed and he scared them and they ran and left but he'll do it again.

Lola Frank (13)

The Joseph Rowntree School, New Earswick

BLOOD FOR BLOOD

I never really belonged in this cruel, twisted world. They killed millions of my kind, and now I'm the sole survivor; I have to seek vengeance.

The most important aspect of my existence disappeared like a lost memory. My family. Death, that's what I saw before me as I slaughtered my enemies - driven by raging anger. Even after all that, I felt incomplete; I was never really satisfied. Was bloodshed the right solution?

Sofia Saabi (13) & Emma Newlands

The Joseph Rowntree School, New Earswick

VENOM GOES UNDERCOVER

I wish I had saved that poor little girl who was only three months old. Everyone thought I was a superhero but now everyone started to boo at me so I went undercover. Someone offered me the job of a hitman but I didn't accept. Soon I was invited to be a valet so I decided to accept. They asked me how much money I wanted so I said I wanted £10,000. They agreed and I accepted the job. I had an idea... I stole all of their cars!

Reagan Smallwood (12)
The Joseph Rowntree School, New Earswick

IT'S ALL ABOUT TRIX

I was never loved, not really anyway. Neither my mum nor dad ever cared about me. Every day my younger sister followed me even in my darkest decisions. I only ever went to the Dark Lord because of them. I only did anything to make them proud but they left me with no other choice but to end up in Azkaban.

I never wanted to kill Sirius or anyone. I really regret everything I did... Hopefully, Harry Potter will defeat Voldemort.

Paige Nichol (11)
The Joseph Rowntree School, New Earswick

SECRET OF THE SHADOW

I did it to be free. When I was young, my parents discovered I was gifted with a power. But every power comes with a price. They hid me from my town, locked me away. Rumours spread like wildfire across the small area, whispers of magical forces I possessed. I couldn't take it anymore. So I used my powers to break free from my parents' grasp. I cursed the little town, swearing I'd get my revenge...

Lizzie Rhodes (12)

The Joseph Rowntree School, New Earswick

POOR HARLEY QUINN

It was Wednesday the 17th of June and it was Harley Quinn's 18th birthday. She got up and got ready for school. She was excited to get all her presents from her friends. Suddenly, her jaw dropped as she walked in and all her friends that she thought would get her loads of gifts were holding a poster, saying, "Ha, ha, nobody got you anything for your birthday."

Lexie Newlove (11)
The Joseph Rowntree School, New Earswick

THE DREAM

One day there was a boy called Luke who suddenly heard a bang on the door so he hid under his bed. Suddenly, he heard heavy breathing. Soon he was found and he was shocked. A Jedi had appeared and they got into a fight. Luke knew who it was... it was Darth Vader. Luke ran but fell dead on the floor. He woke up later and found out it was all just a bad dream.

Jack Stamp
The Joseph Rowntree School, New Earswick

![YoungWriters Est. 1991]

YOUNG WRITERS
INFORMATION

We hope you have enjoyed reading this book – and
that you will continue to in the coming years.

If you're a young writer who enjoys reading and creative
writing, or the parent of an enthusiastic poet or story writer,
do visit our website **www.youngwriters.co.uk**. Here you
will find free competitions, workshops and games, as well
as recommended reads, a poetry glossary and our blog.
There's lots to keep budding writers motivated to write!

If you would like to order further copies of this book,
or any of our other titles, then please give us a
call or order via your online account.

Young Writers
Remus House
Coltsfoot Drive
Peterborough
PE2 9BF
(01733) 890066
info@youngwriters.co.uk

Join in the conversation!
Tips, news, giveaways and much more!

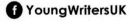 **YoungWritersUK** 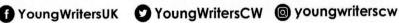 **YoungWritersCW** 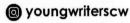 **youngwriterscw**